Super Bunny!

Stephanie Blake's passion for writing and illustrating began in childhood when she created books
for her brothers and sisters as birthday presents. As a child, she also fell in love with the books of
Dr. Seuss, Ludwig Bemelmans, and William Steig. After moving to France, she discovered other writers
and artists whose work continued to inspire her stories and drawings. Stephanie is the
author and illustrator of dozens of books. She lives in Paris, France.

First published in the United States, Great Britain, Canada, Australia, and New Zealand in 2015
by NorthSouth Books, Inc., an imprint of Nord-Süd Verlag AG, CH-8005 Zürich, Switzerland.

Distributed in the United States by NorthSouth Books, Inc., New York 10016.
Library of Congress Cataloging-in-Publication Data is available.

ISBN: 978-0-7358-4223-6
Printed in China by Leo Paper Products Ltd., Heshan, Guangdong, April 2015.
1 3 5 7 9 • 10 8 6 4 2
www.northsouth.com

Stephanie Blake

Super Bunny!

North
South

Once
upon a
time, there
was a little bunny
who thought he was
Super Bunny!
When his mother
told him, "Get up,
little bunny!"
he answered,

"I am
Super Bunny!"

"Not so super,"
said Snowy the cat.

When his
mom asked him,
"What are you going
to do today, little bunny?"
he replied,
"Dear Mother,
I am not a little bunny.
I am Super Bunny!
Super Bunnies
catch bad guys,
you know!"

So that day
Super Bunny
went off in search
of the bad guys.

All of a sudden
he found
a hole
in a tree.
Nothing was
moving inside.

Super Bunny,
who was frightened
of nothing,
hopped into the hole.
But it was very
cold and dark inside.
Suddenly
he started to scream
with all his might.

"Mommy!"

"Mommy! Mommy! Mommy!"

the little bunny yelled. "I've got
a piece of sword
in my finger!"

The little bunny's
mommy went to
look for something
to take out whatever
was stuck in the
little bunny's finger.

When his mommy
asked him, "How did
you do that, little bunny?"
he answered,
"A bad guy
had a sword that was
this BIG!"
"Oh, I see, little bunny."

But as the
needle came closer,
the little bunny
felt something new.
He was scared,
and he hurt.

The little bunny's
mommy took out
the splinter and cried,
"You're the bravest
of all the little bunnies.
You really aren't
scared of anything!"
And the little bunny hollered,
"That's only natural!
I am
Super Bunny!"

When his mommy
asked him,
"Where are you going
with that splinter,
little bunny?"
he answered,

"Oh!
Mother Dear,
this is no splinter.
It is a **Super Sword!**
I'm going to
go after the bad guys,
because
**I'm
Super Bunny!**"